Grace the Glitter Fairy

by Daisy Meadows

illustrated by Georgie Ripper

Join the Rainbow Magic Reading Challenge!

Read the story and collect your fairy points to climb the Reading Rainbow online. Turn to the back of the book for details!

This book is worth 5 points.

RAINBOW magic ®

The Party Fairies

To Ellie Delamere who loves fairies

Special thanks to
Narinder Dhami

ORCHARD BOOKS

First published in Great Britain in 2005 by Orchard Books
This edition published in 2016 by The Watts Publishing Group

3 5 7 9 10 8 6 4 2

© 2016 Rainbow Magic Limited.
© 2016 HIT Entertainment Limited.
Illustrations © Georgie Ripper 2005

HiT entertainment

A CIP catalogue record for this book is available from the British Library.

ISBN 978 1 40834 867 3

Printed in Great Britain

MIX
Paper from
responsible sources
FSC® C104740
FSC
www.fsc.org

The paper and board used in this book are made from wood from responsible sources

Orchard Books
An imprint of Hachette Children's Group
Part of The Watts Publishing Group Limited
Carmelite House, 50 Victoria Embankment, London EC4Y 0DZ

An Hachette UK Company
www.hachette.co.uk
www.hachettechildrens.co.uk

Jack Frost's
Ice Castle

Forest
of
Greenwood

e Park

The Sweet
Shop

Kirsty's
House

Charlotte's
House

Jamie Cooper's
House

A Very Special Party Invitation

Our gracious King and gentle Queen
Are loved by fairies all.
One thousand years have they ruled well,
Through troubles great and small.

In honour of their glorious reign
A party has been planned,
To celebrate their jubilee
Throughout all Fairyland.

The party is a royal surprise,
We hope they'll be delighted.
So shine your wand and press your dress...
For you have been invited!

RSVP: HRH THE FAIRY GODMOTHER

Contents

A Party Afoot

"Isn't it a beautiful day?" Kirsty Tate said happily, looking up at the deep blue sky. "I'm so glad you're staying here for a whole week, Rachel."

Kirsty was sitting on the grass in the Tates' back garden, making a daisy chain with her best friend, Rachel Walker. Pearl, Kirsty's black and white kitten,

was snoozing in a patch of sunshine
in the middle of the path.

"You know, Rachel," Kirsty went
on, picking another daisy. "This is the
perfect day for—"

"A party!" Rachel broke in, knowing
exactly what Kirsty was going to say.

Kirsty nodded, a frown on her face.
"Let's hope horrid Jack Frost's goblins
don't spoil someone's special day."

"The Party Fairies will do their best to stop them," Rachel replied in a determined voice. "And so will we."

Rachel and Kirsty had a wonderful secret which no one else in the whole human world knew about. They were best friends with the fairies! So far, the girls had helped the Rainbow Fairies and the Weather Fairies against Jack Frost's evil spells. Now it was the turn of the Party Fairies.

"Isn't it just like mean old Jack Frost to want to spoil everyone's fun?" said Kirsty. "He can't stop causing trouble, even though he's been banished to his ice castle."

"If he hadn't been such a pest, he could have come to the surprise party for the Fairy King and Queen's 1000th jubilee," Rachel pointed out.

The girls had been invited to the Fairyland party themselves, and they had been very excited about it – until they found out that Jack Frost was determined to have a party of his own. His goblins were causing trouble at human parties, so that the Party Fairies would appear to put things right. Then the goblins would try to steal the fairies' magic party bags for Jack Frost to use at his party.

"Well, we managed to keep Cherry the Cake Fairy and Melodie the Music Fairy's party bags safe," Kirsty said, adding another daisy to her chain. "We'll just have to keep our eyes open."

"And our ears," added Rachel.

Suddenly, there was a scrabbling noise behind the hedge. "OW!" someone muttered. "That hurt."

"Who was that?" gasped Rachel. "Do you think it was a goblin?"

Kirsty grinned and shook her head. "It's OK," she said. "It sounds like Mr Cooper, our next-door neighbour."

At that moment, Mr Cooper popped his head over the hedge. He was a tall, thin man with a cheerful smile. "Sorry, Kirsty," he said, "did I startle you?

I pricked my finger on the rosebush."
He held up a small parcel wrapped in
shiny blue paper. "I'm trying to hide
these presents around the garden for the
treasure hunt this afternoon."

"Treasure hunt?" repeated Rachel,
looking puzzled.

Mr Cooper nodded. "Yes, it's my son
Jamie's birthday today," he replied.
"He's five and we're having a party."

A party! Rachel and
Kirsty glanced
at each other
in excitement.

"We've got ten
children coming,"
Mr Cooper went on.
"And we've hired a clown called
Mr Chuckles. Jamie is really excited."
He smiled and shook his head.
"It's going to be a lot of hard
work, though."

Rachel nudged Kirsty, who knew
exactly what her friend was thinking.

"Maybe Rachel and I could come
over and give you and Mrs Cooper
a hand?" Kirsty suggested.

"Yes, we'd love to," Rachel
added eagerly.

Mr Cooper's face lit up. "That's very kind of you," he beamed. "Jamie would love that. The guests are arriving at three o'clock, so could you come at two?"

"Of course we will," Rachel and Kirsty said together.

Mr Cooper gave them a grateful smile, and went off to hide some more parcels.

Kirsty turned to Rachel, her eyes wide with excitement. "Do you think a goblin will turn up and try to spoil Jamie's party?" she asked.

"I don't know," Rachel replied. "But if one does, we'll be ready for him!"

Decorating Difficulties

"This is going to be fun," Kirsty
grinned, as she rang the Coopers'
doorbell. "Jamie is really sweet. It'll
be a bit noisy, though, with him and
all his friends running around enjoying
themselves."

"Maybe they'll frighten the goblins
away!" Rachel said with a laugh.

The front door opened. A small boy with exactly the same cheerful smile as Mr Cooper stood in the hallway.

"Hello, Kirsty," Jamie called eagerly. "Are you and your friend here to help with my party?"

"Yes, we are," Kirsty replied, smiling and handing Jamie a parcel. "Happy birthday."

Jamie tore off the wrapping paper excitedly and beamed when he saw the bright red car inside. "Thank you! Come on," he said, taking Kirsty's hand. "Me and Mummy are putting up decorations in the lounge."

Rachel and Kirsty followed him down the hallway. Mrs Cooper was standing on a chair, pinning a HAPPY BIRTHDAY banner to the wall.

"Hello, Kirsty," she smiled. "And it's Rachel, isn't it? It's so kind of you to help out. Thank you."

"Mum!" Jamie was dancing around the lounge, waving his new car. "Look what Kirsty and Rachel gave me! And can we put up the streamers now? Can we?"

"There's still an hour to go and he's already fizzing with excitement," Mrs Cooper said, laughing. "Would you girls be able to put up the streamers and balloons, please, while I go and help Jamie's dad finish off the food?" She pointed to a folded, gold-coloured paper tablecloth, and some bowls and plates which were on the table. "And if you have time, could you lay the table, too?"

"Of course we can," Rachel replied.

Mrs Cooper thanked the girls and hurried off to the kitchen.

Jamie grabbed the box of decorations from the sofa. "Daddy bought some new extra-long streamers," said Jamie proudly. "They're gold and silver – look!"

He began unrolling one of the streamers. But before he had got very far, a piece about fifty centimetres long dropped off and floated to the ground.

"Oh!" Jamie gasped.

"I'm sure the rest of it is OK," Rachel said quickly.

"Keep going, Jamie."

But as Jamie unrolled the streamer, more lengths of brightly-coloured paper fell off. Rachel opened the other packets, but those streamers had been spoiled in exactly the same way.

"It's just as if someone has cut the streamers and then rolled them back up again," Kirsty whispered to Rachel.

Rachel nodded solemnly. "Do you think it could be goblin mischief?" she asked.

Jamie was looking close to tears.

"They're too short!" he wailed.

"Don't worry, Jamie,"
Kirsty said, giving him
a hug. "I've got just
the thing to fix this.
I won't be long."

Kirsty ran home
and found a big
roll of sparkly, blue
sticky-tape, which was
left over from Christmas. Then
she went back to the Coopers' house
and showed it to Jamie. "Look,"
she said, beginning to stick the pieces
of one of the streamers together.
"Now you'll have stripy gold, silver
and blue streamers."

Jamie's face lit up. "They look even
better now!" he declared happily.

The three of them quickly stuck the rest
of the streamers together and then Rachel
and Kirsty began to pin them up around
the room. They had just finished when
there was a ring at the doorbell.

"That'll be Mr Chuckles," Mrs
Cooper called from the kitchen. "Could
you let him in, please, Kirsty?"

"I think Jamie has beaten me to it,"
Kirsty chuckled, as Jamie dashed past
her into the hall.

Rachel and Kirsty followed him, and found the clown standing on the doorstep, smiling down at Jamie. He wore a bright blue, baggy suit and a blue bowler hat.

"You must be the birthday boy," he said.

"Where's your big red nose and your big clown shoes, Mr Chuckles?" Jamie wanted to know.

Rachel and Kirsty smiled.

"Ah, well, I'm not quite ready yet," Mr Chuckles explained. "It's difficult to drive my van in big clown shoes."

Looking as if he was about to burst with
excitement, Jamie ran to tell his mum
about the clown.

Meanwhile, Mr Chuckles turned to
Rachel and Kirsty. "Is it OK if I set up
my stuff in the lounge?" he asked.

Kirsty nodded. "Yes, we've almost
finished decorating," she replied. "We've
just got the balloons to blow up."

The clown opened the back of his van

and began to unload his props, while
the girls went back into the lounge. But
to their dismay, the streamers which
they had so carefully pinned up earlier
had all fallen down. Now they lay in
heaps on the floor.

"This has to be the work of one of
Jack Frost's goblins!" Rachel said
crossly, grabbing a streamer. "He must
be here somewhere."

"Quick, let's get these back up or
Jamie will be upset," Kirsty said, picking
up the sticky-tape.

The girls worked fast and got the
streamers back in place before Jamie
came bouncing into the room.

"We're going to blow up the balloons now, Jamie," said Kirsty, opening one of the packets. "Which colour shall we start with?"

"Gold!" Jamie called eagerly.

Kirsty began to blow air into the long gold balloon. But although she huffed and puffed and got red in the face, the balloon wouldn't inflate. It remained as flat as a pancake.

"There's a hole in it," Rachel said, peering closely at the balloon.

The girls exchanged a look. They were both thinking exactly the same thing.

"The goblin again!" Kirsty whispered. Quickly, she and Rachel checked all the other balloons. There were holes in all of them! Jamie's bottom lip was trembling. "Are all the balloons spoiled?" he asked in a small voice.

At that moment, Mr Chuckles came into the lounge carrying a large wooden box. "Is it balloons you need?" he asked. "I've got some spares." He put his hand into his pocket and pulled out a handful of different-coloured balloons. "I use them to make my balloon animals."

Kirsty and Rachel were very relieved to see Jamie smiling again. Quickly, they blew up the balloons and hung them around the French windows at the far end of the room.

Suddenly, the doorbell rang. Jamie peeped out of the front window. "It's Matthew, my best friend!" he shouted excitedly. "And Katie and Andy and Ben. It's time for my party to start!" And he dashed out to meet his guests.

"Goodness me, I must go to the
bathroom and put my clown make-up
on," said Mr Chuckles. He grabbed a
small case and left the room.

POP! POP! POP!

Kirsty and Rachel jumped and turned
round. The balloons they had just put
up were bursting, one by one.

"I'm starting to get very fed up with that goblin," Rachel said crossly.

"So am I," Kirsty agreed. "We need to find him and put a stop to his tricks!"

The doorbell was ringing again as more guests arrived, and the girls could hear them chattering excitedly in the hall. They didn't have much time to find and stop the goblin.

Then they heard Mr Cooper's voice. "Follow me out to the garden, kids," he was saying. "We're going to have a treasure hunt!"

There was a loud cheer as the children hurried after him, and Rachel and Kirsty looked at each other in relief.

"Let's search the room," Kirsty
suggested. "We might be able to deal
with the goblin while everyone's in the
garden."

But just as they began their search,
Rachel groaned with dismay and
clutched Kirsty's arm.

"What is it?" Kirsty whispered.

"Look!" Rachel said, pointing
towards the French windows.
"Outside in the garden."

Kirsty peered through the
glass to see a sparkling
pink shape flying swiftly
through the air. It
was zooming straight
through the garden,
towards the French
windows of the lounge.

"Oh!" Kirsty gasped. "It's Grace the Glitter Fairy!"

"Yes," said Rachel anxiously. "And the children are going out into the garden. They'll all see her unless we do something — and fast!"

Saving Grace

"We have to go outside and warn her," Kirsty said.

"What about the goblin?" Rachel asked.

"This is more important," Kirsty replied, opening the French windows. She and Rachel rushed outside, waving their arms madly to get Grace's attention.

Grace saw them straightaway and waved her sparkling pink wand at them. She had long, straight, glossy blonde hair, and she wore a glittering rose-coloured dress, which shimmered in the sunshine. The hem of the dress was red and cut into handkerchief points. The floaty skirt swirled around her legs as she hovered in mid-air.

"Hello, girls," she called, "It's good to see you—"

"Grace, you have to hide!" Kirsty burst out, without even saying hello. "The party guests are about to come out into the garden any minute!"

Before Grace could say anything, they heard the back door open.

"So that's what you have to do, kids," Mr Cooper was saying. "Off you go."

Grace looked alarmed as all the children came galloping out of the back door. "Thanks for warning me, girls," she gasped. And she fluttered out of sight behind a garden urn filled with flowers.

The children were running all round
the garden now, screaming with
excitement. Two little girls came over
to where Kirsty and Rachel were
standing, and began to search for
presents there.

"Er, I think Mr Cooper hid most of
the presents down the bottom of the
garden," Rachel said quickly. She
didn't want the little girls poking
around and finding Grace.

One of the girls ran off straight away,
but the other one frowned.
"I can see something
sparkly behind
that pot," she said
stubbornly, pointing
at the urn. "It might
be one of the presents."

"Oh, no," Kirsty said, thinking fast.
She bent down and picked Grace up,
keeping the fairy out
of sight in her hand.
Then she popped
her in her pocket.
"That's just
an empty
sweetie wrapper."

"We'll put it in the
bin with the rubbish," Rachel added.

The girl looked disappointed and ran off after her friend. Kirsty and Rachel sighed with relief.

"Rubbish?" Grace said, poking her head out of Kirsty's pocket. She looked a bit flustered and her hair was all messy. "That's nice!"

"Sorry, Grace," Kirsty said soothingly. "We didn't mean it."

"There's a goblin here," Rachel told Grace, as the little fairy smoothed down her hair. "He's been ruining all the party decorations in the lounge."

"Well, we'll soon put a stop to that!" Grace declared, looking outraged.

"Where is he?"

"We don't know," Kirsty replied. "We were just about to start looking for him, when we saw you coming."

Grace nodded. "Well, now I can help you find him," she said, smiling. "Lead the way!"

As Kirsty led the way through the French windows into the lounge, she suddenly gasped and caught Rachel's arm. "Look, there!" she breathed. "Behind the curtain."

Rachel and Grace looked at the long blue curtains hanging either side of the French windows, and immediately saw what Kirsty had spotted – behind one of them, there was a definite goblin-shape!

An Uninvited Guest

They all stared at the goblin bulge behind the curtain. They saw it shift once or twice. The goblin was obviously getting a bit fed up.

Kirsty beckoned Rachel and Grace to follow her to the other end of the room. "We need to do something right now," Kirsty whispered.

"Before Jamie and his friends come in from the garden."

"Yes, but what?" Grace queried, biting her lip anxiously.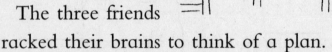

The three friends racked their brains to think of a plan.

"We could creep up on the goblin and grab him while he's wrapped in the curtain," Rachel suggested. "It shouldn't be too difficult. He's quite small." Rachel knew that Jack Frost's magic could make the goblins much bigger and scarier when they were in the human world, but as the Fairy King and Queen had taken Jack Frost's magic away for one year, the goblins were their normal size.

"Then Grace can quickly magic him away to Fairyland," Rachel added.

Grace nodded enthusiastically, but Kirsty looked worried. "He'll try to fight his way out," she said. "What if he ruins the curtain?"

"Well, it's made of really thick material," Rachel pointed out. "I don't think the goblin will be able to do much damage."

"And I can fix it with Fairy magic once I'm back in Fairyland," put in Grace. "And then I'll whiz back here and magic it into place for you, too."

"OK, let's give it a try," Kirsty agreed.

She and Rachel crept cautiously towards the French windows, with Grace fluttering alongside. They had nearly reached the goblin, when the lounge door suddenly opened and Mrs Cooper appeared, laden with plates of food.

Quick as a flash,
Grace darted
into Kirsty's
pocket, out
of sight.

"Ah, girls,"
said Jamie's mum.
"Could you possibly
give me a hand with these snacks?"

Rachel and Kirsty exchanged an
agonised look, but there was nothing
they could do.

"Yes, of course," Kirsty replied
politely, and the girls hurried to help
Mrs Cooper set the plates down on the
dining table.

"As soon as the children have finished
the treasure hunt, we'll bring them
in here," Mrs Cooper told the girls.

"They can have a snack before they watch Mr Chuckles, and then after his show, we'll have tea."

The girls nodded and Mrs Cooper headed back to the kitchen.

As soon as she had gone, Grace fluttered out of Kirsty's pocket and the girls turned back to tackle the goblin. But it was too late!

"Oh, no!" gasped Rachel, as she looked around the room. All the streamers lay on the floor again. The decorations were ruined. But, worse than that, the goblin-shape behind the curtain had vanished!

"Well, at least I can set these decorations to rights," Grace said, reaching into her pocket for her party bag.

But Kirsty stopped her. "No, you mustn't," she said in a low voice. "That's exactly what the goblin wants you to do. He's hiding somewhere – just waiting for the chance to snatch your party bag!"

Goblin Trap!

At that very moment, the three friends heard a scrabbling noise behind the sofa!

"The goblin must be hiding over there," Rachel whispered excitedly, pointing to the sofa. "And he's heard us talking about the party bag."

Kirsty's face lit up. "That's it!" she whispered. "We'll use Grace's party bag as bait to catch the goblin."

"I know how we can grab him, too," Rachel added quietly. She pointed at the paper tablecloth, which Mrs Cooper had bought for the party. "We'll wrap him up in the tablecloth instead of the curtain, and then Grace can still whisk him off to Fairyland!"

"Good idea," Grace whispered. "We'll hide behind that armchair, and catch him red-handed." Then she spoke again in a louder voice. "My party bag's so heavy, girls," she said with a wink. "It's because I've got so much magic fairy dust in it."

"Why don't you put it down on the coffee table?" Rachel suggested, glancing at the sofa.

"Then you can come into the kitchen with us, and we'll show you Jamie's beautiful birthday cake," added Kirsty, picking up the shiny, gold-coloured tablecloth. "It's in the shape of a steam train."

"OK," Grace agreed. She pulled her sparkly blue party bag from her pocket, and placed it carefully on the coffee table. "Let's go then."

But instead of leaving the room, they
all tiptoed over to the armchair, and
hid behind it. It was a bit of a squash.
Kirsty and Rachel were too big to both
fit behind the chair.

"Rachel, your feet are sticking out,"
Grace whispered. "Wait a moment."

She twirled her blue
wand in the air and
there was a sparkle
of fairy dust. In a
second, Rachel and
Kirsty had shrunk to
fairy-size, with glittering
wings on their backs. As tiny fairies,
it was easy for all three friends to fit
behind the armchair. Kirsty fluttered
her wings happily.

Grace looked
pleased. "That's
better," she
said, glancing
at the sofa.
"And we're
just in time.
Here he comes…"

The goblin poked his head round the edge of the sofa to see if the coast was clear. Then he stepped out, a big grin on his mean face. His beady little eyes gleamed as he saw the party bag lying on the coffee table, and he hurried to pick it up. "Jack Frost will be really pleased with me," the goblin chortled smugly.

But as he reached for the party bag, Grace, Kirsty and Rachel zoomed out of their hiding place, each holding a corner of the tablecloth.

"Get him!" Rachel yelled.

They hovered above the surprised
goblin, and dropped the tablecloth right
over him. He gave a shout of fury as it
covered him completely from head to toe.

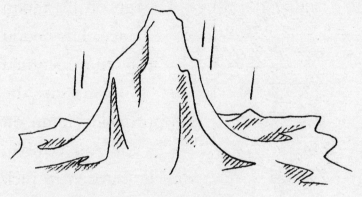

"It worked!" cried Kirsty.

"Now, let's wrap him up more
tightly," Grace said.

But before they do so, the goblin
began to rip the tablecloth to shreds!

All Wrapped Up!

"He's tearing his way out!" Kirsty exclaimed. "What shall we do?"

Rachel looked round, spotted the streamers on the floor and had an idea. She grabbed the end of one of them, and flew swiftly round and round the goblin, tying him up.

"Quick, Kirsty!" Grace called, as she saw what Rachel was doing. "Grab a streamer."

"Stop it!" the goblin called crossly. He tried to fight his way out, but Grace and the girls were wrapping him up too quickly. A few minutes later he couldn't move. He looked just like an Egyptian mummy.

"Ohhh!" the goblin groaned sulkily.

"Serves you right," Rachel told him, as Grace rescued her precious party bag.

Meanwhile, Kirsty had fluttered over to the French windows to check on the treasure hunt.

"OK, kids, you've found all the presents," Mr Cooper was saying. "Now it's time to see Mr Chuckles, the clown."

"Jamie and his friends are coming in now, Grace," Kirsty called. "You'd better go."

Grace turned to the goblin. "And you're coming with me," she laughed. She waved her wand, and the moaning, grumbling goblin disappeared in a cloud of sparkling fairy dust.

"Goodbye, girls, and thank you,"
Grace said. She gave
them a hug, and
with a wave of her
wand, made them
human-sized again.
Then Kirsty
remembered the decorations.
"Grace, can you help?" she asked,
pointing at the streamers and balloons.

Grace nodded and smiled. She tipped up
her party bag, and emptied all the fairy
dust into the lounge. Tiny, shining
diamonds whirled and swirled around the
room, spinning into every corner.

When the magic dust had cleared, Kirsty
and Rachel were delighted to see that the
walls were festooned with glittering,
rainbow-coloured streamers and balloons.

There was even a new, gold, paper tablecloth, and when Kirsty and Rachel spread it out on the table, they saw that it was shinier than before and covered with a sprinkling of gleaming silver stars.

"Thank you!" the girls cried in amazement.

Grace gave a silvery laugh, waved her wand and disappeared, just as the children charged in led by Mr Cooper. They all stopped and stared in amazement at the fabulous decorations.

"Wow!" Jamie gasped. "Look what Kirsty and Rachel have done, Dad!"

"It's fantastic, girls," said Mr Cooper gratefully.

Rachel and Kirsty beamed at each other, and sat down with the party guests to watch Mr Chuckles perform. The clown was very funny and had everyone in fits of laughter with a giant, water-squirting sunflower. Rachel and Kirsty enjoyed it just as much as Jamie and his friends.

At the end of the show, Mr Chuckles
told them he was going to make some
balloon animals. When he opened his
bag and pulled out a handful of
balloons, there was a gasp of wonder.
They were the most wonderful,
colourful balloons anyone had ever
seen – and some were even striped and
spotted with animal-print designs.

Mr Chuckles stared at them in delight. "I didn't even know I had these," he muttered.

Rachel and Kirsty smiled. They knew where those balloons had come from – Grace the Glitter Fairy!

Mr Chuckles began to twist and tie the balloons together. He made an elephant first, which he gave to Jamie. Then he made a lovely giraffe and a zebra.

"These are for the two girls who put up these beautiful decorations," Mr Chuckles said. He bowed, and presented the giraffe to Rachel and the zebra to Kirsty. The girls were thrilled.

And so was somebody else...

"This is my best birthday ever!" Jamie beamed, as the clown began to make animals for all the other children.

"And we've saved another Party Fairy and her party bag," Rachel whispered happily to Kirsty. "Hurray!"

Now Rachel and Kirsty
must help...

Honey the Sweet Fairy

Read on for a sneak peek...

It was a lovely, sunny day, and Mr
and Mrs Tate had set lunch outside in
the garden. As Kirsty and her best
friend, Rachel Walker, sat down to eat,
Mrs Tate suddenly groaned aloud.

"I knew there was something else
I meant to get from the shops this
morning," she cried. "Gran's toffees! I
promised I'd take her some this evening,
and I completely forgot to buy them."

Kirsty put down her sandwich.
"Don't worry, Mum. We'll go to Mrs
Twist's Sweet Shop after lunch for

you," she suggested. She glanced at Rachel. "What do you think?"

"Sure," Rachel said. "I've always got time to go to the sweet shop!"

The two girls smiled at each other. Rachel was staying with the Tates for a whole week. She and Kirsty had met one summer holiday, and they had been good friends ever since. Somehow, whenever the pair of them got together, they always seemed to have the most wonderful adventures. Fairy adventures!

"That reminds me," Mr Tate said. "I saw in the local newspaper that Mrs Twist is retiring. Her daughter's taking over the sweet shop from tomorrow. As this is her last day, Mrs Twist is throwing a party for all her customers." He winked at Kirsty and Rachel.

"I read something about there being plenty of free sweets up for grabs, too!

Kirsty nudged Rachel at once. "Sweets a party," she repeated. "How exciting!"

"We love parties," Rachel agreed, with a grin.

The two friends shared a secret. They had been busy all week helping the Party Fairies of Fairyland! The fairies were preparing a surprise celebration for the Fairy King and Queen's 1000th jubilee – but wicked Jack Frost had plans for his own rival party. All week, he'd been sending his goblins into the human world to disrupt people's parties...

Read Honey the Sweet Fairy
to find out what adventures are in store for Kirsty and Rachel!

Meet the
Friendship Fairies

When Jack Frost steals the Friendship Fairies' magical objects, BFFs everywhere are in trouble! Can Rachel and Kirsty help save the magic of friendship?

www.rainbowmagicbooks.co.uk

Calling all parents, carers and teachers!
The Rainbow Magic fairies are here to help
your child enter the magical world of reading.
Whatever reading stage they are at, there's
a Rainbow Magic book for everyone!
Here is Lydia the Reading Fairy's guide to
supporting your child's journey at all levels.

Starting Out

Our Rainbow Magic Beginner Readers are perfect for first-time readers who are just beginning to develop reading skills and confidence. Approved by teachers, they contain a full range of educational levelling, as well as lively full-colour illustrations.

Developing Readers

Rainbow Magic Early Readers contain longer stories and wider vocabulary for building stamina and growing confidence. These are adaptations of our most popular Rainbow Magic stories, specially developed for younger readers in conjunction with an Early Years reading consultant, with full-colour illustrations.

Going Solo

The Rainbow Magic chapter books – a mixture of series and one-off specials – contain accessible writing to encourage your child to venture into reading independently. These highly collectible and much-loved magical stories inspire a love of reading to last a lifetime.

www.rainbowmagicbooks.co.uk

"Rainbow Magic got my daughter reading chapter books. Great sparkly covers, cute fairies and traditional stories full of magic that she found impossible to put down" – Mother of Edie (6 years)

"Florence LOVES the Rainbow Magic books. She really enjoys reading now" Mother of Florence (6 years)

The Rainbow Magic Reading Challenge

Well done, fairy friend – you have completed the book!
This book was worth 5 points.

See how far you have climbed on the **Reading Rainbow**
on the Rainbow Magic website below.

The more books you read, the more points you will get,
and the closer you will be to becoming a Fairy Princess!

How to get your Reading Rainbow
1. Cut out the coin below
2. Go to the Rainbow Magic website
3. Download and print out your poster
4. Add your coin and climb up the Reading Rainbow!

There's all this and lots more at
www.rainbowmagicbooks.co.uk

You'll find activities, competitions, stories, a special
newsletter and complete profiles of all the
Rainbow Magic fairies. Find a fairy with your name!